DEDICATION

This book is dedicated to YOU and all of your efforts to make the world a better place.

♥ In Gratitude ♥

Printed by CreateSpace, An Amazon.com Company

www.CreateSpace.com

CreateSpace, Charleston SC

Copy editors Patti Newman and Jon Newman

Image editors Raine Dudley and Charles Shelton

Book design Raine Dudley, Lisa Ann Helmly, and Margaret Ann Rowland

Princess Loggerhead's Gratitude Journey

LoGGeRHeaD Turtle NestiNG ARea

Written by
Lisa Ann
Helmly

Illustrated by
Margaret Ann
Rowland

In the oceans below, there are many different sea creatures doing their duties as they prepare for their destiny. Princess Loggerhead is one of those wonders of nature proud to be chosen to have other turtles and contribute to the loggerhead population. She takes her job seriously because she knows that her species is becoming endangered and if this happens, this ancient reptile could become extinct.

Princess Loggerhead had a strong feeling come over her that she could not ignore. Her instinct was letting her know that it was time to say farewell to her fellow family of sea creatures and begin her journey. Although she was a thousand miles away, Princess Loggerhead began to travel the distance back to her favorite nesting spot, Folly Beach, South Carolina.

Every two to three years Princess Loggerhead would sense those internal signals and head to this coastal land. As nature would have it, she would mate, travel to shore, and then prepare to lay her eggs. This place was the same location where her mother had nested and had Princess Loggerhead, along with many other little turtle hatchlings.

As Princess Loggerhead approached the coastline, she felt a sense of peace come over her. She noticed how clean the beach was as the seagulls foraged for food. It was obvious to her that the people of Folly Beach were taking pride in the environment by doing their part to help make this beach clean and safe for all to enjoy.

Upon arriving at Folly Beach, Princess Loggerhead was greeted by a dragonfly. She smiled and said, "What a nice day to visit my favorite nesting spot and be welcomed by the colors of you."

The dragonfly replied, "Much obliged!"

"Looks like the people around here have sure been busy maintaining this place and steadily making improvements," commented Princess Loggerhead.

The dragonfly smiled back while saying, "Oh yes, the people here have made great strides in protecting the environment. They also continue to promote the safety of the Loggerhead Turtle, too."

Princess Loggerhead replied, "And how might that be, my new dragonfly friend? Please tell me more."

The dragonfly fluttered around joyfully while responding, "Well, hang around for a while. It gets real interesting around here with fun-filled activities and even a gratitude parade."

"A gratitude parade? You don't say! Maybe I will take you up on that and see for myself," Princess Loggerhead replied quite curiously.

Princess Loggerhead began to meander her way down the beach and seek out a perfect spot to lay her eggs. While approaching the sand dunes, she noticed how some nesting areas had been carefully taped off as though they were being protected. The sea turtle activists of Folly Beach had marked these nesting sites to provide a safe haven for the eggs to peacefully incubate until time to hatch.

By designating where the turtles had laid their eggs, the humans would know not to disturb the nests. They could also keep an eye out for any activities from animal predators that might be looking for food. Princess Loggerhead was grateful for their efforts in preserving the nesting sites so that new life can happen.

Princess Loggerhead continued to explore the beach. She noticed that there were more beach houses, streetlights, and buildings than she had remembered from past visits. Since turtles follow natural skylight from the moon and the stars as they make their way to the sea after nesting or hatching, she was concerned that the lights from man-made sources might confuse the turtles as to which direction to go.

Suddenly, she looked up and a sign caught her eye… "Lights Out-Turtle Watch!" Princess Loggerhead sighed with relief to see that once again the citizens of Folly Beach were looking out for the best interests of these ancient reptiles and their offspring.

From around the corner and down the street joyful noises of laughter and music could be heard. A festive crab came scurrying by just glowing with excitement.

"Where are you off to in such a hurry, dear lad?" Princess Loggerhead asked.

"It's The Gratitude Parade! Come join the fun, fun, fun," the silly crab replied.

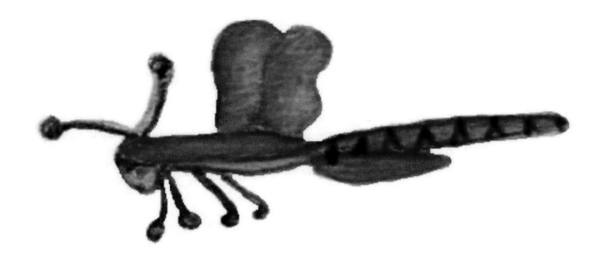

Princess Loggerhead decided to stroll into town and see what the commotion was all about.

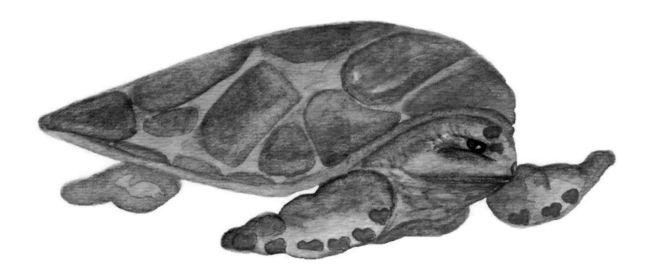

The local businesses and people of the community were putting on "The Gratitude Parade."

Luckily for her, the festivities had just begun.

They wanted to celebrate something good going on in the world, such as all the efforts of the townspeople in leaving a positive footprint on the environment.

Princess Loggerhead was overcome with appreciation for the work of the citizens of Folly Beach in looking out for the safety of these miraculous sea creatures that date back to the days of the dinosaurs. After thinking about everything involved, she had an epiphany. She realized that without the actions of the townspeople, the Loggerhead Turtle would become extinct. Her work as a mother turtle was her destiny. It was a job she was born to do. The work of the townspeople was kindness and compassion in action for it was a job that they chose to do. Princess Loggerhead felt warm fuzzies knowing that the world is a better place for having people in it who care.

After the Gratitude Parade, Princess Loggerhead settled in to complete her nesting season. Although she felt a kinship with the community of Folly Beach, she knew that her life was meant to be lived amongst the other sea creatures where her spirit felt a belonging.

"Go ahead little loggerheads, just follow the light. Sometimes we just need a little help finding our way home," the good friends shared as they encouraged the hatchlings to head toward the brightest horizon.